Mommy & Daddy's
Christmas
Treat

Written by C.L. Holliday-Firmin

Edited by J. Firmin

Illustrated by Gull Zareen

ISBN: 979-8-9853615-0-6 (paperback)

ISBN: 979-8-9853615-1-3 (ebook)

Library of Congress Control Number: 2021924150

CJAA PUBLISHING

Washington, DC

This book is dedicated to my loving husband, darling son, and devoted family. Thank you for your enthusiasm, patience, support, and encouragement I needed to finally share my work with the world. You are forever my inspiration.

It was the evening before Christmas and all through the house, was family laughing, and talking, and dancing about.

Grandma ate the gingerbread and chocolate chip cookies she placed on a tray. Children were playing, hoping Santa was on his way.

The table was set with dinner, desserts, and holiday decor. The room was decked with mistletoe, candy canes and more.

A burst of Christmas you might say, even snowflakes in the air. There were reindeer, ornaments, and lights twinkling everywhere.

Daddy nestled with Mommy, snug in her chair, knowing their newest present would soon be there. Daddy said to Mommy, "I love you honey." "I love you more," she replied, as he rubbed her tummy.

They had been preparing for a year and some months, checking their list twice to cover their baby's needs and wants.

Daddy built the dresser and crib with care, while Mommy washed and folded clothes, baby would wear.

Mommy's favorite Christmas song played as she looked at Daddy. "It's time," she assured, "go grab baby's bag please."

Daddy's eyes brightened, then pecked her cheek after hearing the news. The family was delighted to know the new baby will arrive soon.

After Daddy kissed Mommy, by the tree with the star, they went hand and hand, out the door, and straight to the car.

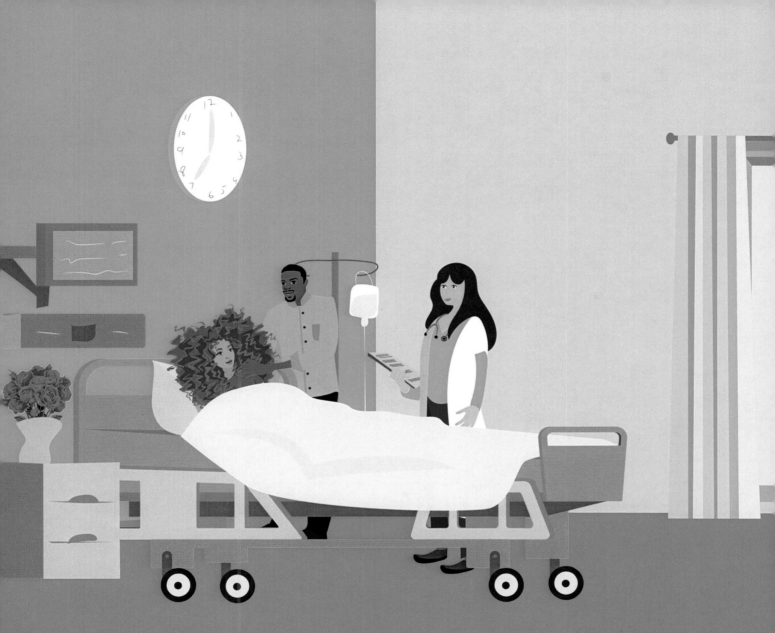

The hospital wasn't far, thank goodness for that. "Mommy and baby are doing very well," said the doctor, "we're right on track."

Cousins upon cousins, were counting down for a glance. There were two sets of grandparents, uncles and aunts.

"The baby will soon be here!" Uncle shouted with joy. "Get my wallet and keys I need to buy another toy!"

Daddy looked at the clock because so much time had passed. He couldn't wait another moment to see his son at last.

Mommy leaned from her bed and hugged Daddy tight. She professed, " This is it, I can feel he's coming tonight."

"Merry Christmas everyone," the doctor
said with glee, "Congratulations, you two,
on your 1st born baby!"

We stared at each other as we held you in our
arms. We kissed you, and we cuddled with
you, to keep you warm.

The next day, as we were leaving, we said our goodbyes. On the drive home, we sang you a lullaby.

"Welcome home little one," Daddy beamed while sipping his cider. Our hearts were overjoyed as we all snuggled by the fire.

From your curious brown eyes, to your cute little feet, Mommy and Daddy love you, our darling Christmas treat.

About the author

C. L. Holliday-Firmin is a writer that has a playful sense of humor, with a whimsical vision of the world.

New to the children's books genre, but not new to writing, this poet is stepping out of the box to share delightful stories after becoming a new parent.

Born on Christmas Day, it is no surprise her first book is Christmas related.

Be on the look out for more short stories parents and children will absolutely love to read again and again.

Made in United States
North Haven, CT
27 January 2022